STORIES FROM
HILLTOP
HOSPITAL

NICHOLAS ALLAN

Hutchinson
London Sydney Auckland Johannesburg

First published in 1997

3 5 7 9 10 8 6 4 2

Text and illustrations © Nicholas Allan

Nicholas Allan has asserted his right under
the Copyright, Designs and Patents Acts, 1988,
to be identified as the author and illustrator of this work

First published in the United Kingdom in 1997 by
Hutchinson Children's Books
The Random House Group Limited
20 Vauxhall Bridge Road, London SW1V 2SA

Random House Australia (Pty) Limited
20 Alfred Street, Milsons Point, Sydney,
New South Wales 2061, Australia

Random House New Zealand Limited
18 Poland Road, Glenfield,
Auckland 10, New Zealand

Random House South Africa (Pty) Limited
Endulini, 5A Jubilee Road, Parktown 2193, South Africa

The Random House Group Limited Reg. No. 954009

www.randomhouse.co.uk

A CIP catalogue record for this book is available from the British Library

Papers used by The Random House Group Ltd are natural, recyclable products
made from wood grown in sustainable forests.
The manufacturing processes conform to the environmental
regulations of the country of origin.

ISBN: 0 09 176618 4

Printed and bound in Great Britain by
Creative Print and Design
(Wales), Ebbw Vale, Gwent

CONTENTS

To Marta and Peter

SURGEON SALLY'S DAY OFF

Birdsong floated through the open window of the bedroom as Surgeon Sally woke at 6 am sharp. It was a bright spring morning, and she was gloomy. She had remembered it was her day off.

Surgeon Sally loved her work; she was lost without it. She thought of all her colleagues busy at Hilltop Hospital, and how she wouldn't see them for at least another twenty-six hours. There were:

Dr Matthews, so clever at making the patients better, even if he wasn't the tidiest doctor in the world;

Staff Nurse Kitty, kind yet efficient, who could always find a warm bed for a new patient;

Dr Atticus, the anaesthetist, who never slept on the job, though he seemed to sleep the rest of the time;

Clare and Arthur, the two lab mice, who mixed up all the medicines for the patients at Hilltop, and finally . . .

the two Teds, Hilltop's trusty ambulance drivers.

Yes, they'll all be there, working away, while I'm stuck at home, thought Surgeon Sally. What am I going to do, she wondered, without a single operation to perform all day? Not even an in-growing claw to dig out.

She couldn't tidy the house because it was already tidy, as spotless as an operating theatre. She lay in bed inspecting the polished mahogany wardrobe, the glittering windows, and the shiny leaves on her plant. At least, she thought, she could enjoy a long lie-in. But by 6.07 am she was, as usual, submerged in her large bath.

'Soap,' she ordered.

'Soap,' she repeated, handing herself the soap.

'Apply soap,' she said.

'Applying soap.'

By 6.19 am she was down in the kitchen slicing bread with surgical precision. After breakfast, at 6.37 am, she loaded plates, knives, cup and saucer into the dish-washer.

'Sterilize instruments,' she ordered, pressing a button.

Then she sat there, head on paws – bored. 6.49 am, said the kitchen clock.

'Only another twenty-five hours and eleven minutes until work,' she murmured. It was also only

7

another twenty-five hours and eleven minutes before she would see Dr Matthews again, although she didn't know why she thought that. She gazed out of the window at her tidy garden with its hedges as trim as a cat's fur and the lawn of newly cut grass, and finally at the far wall. Suddenly her little eyes gleamed; her paws flexed itchily.

'Prepare instruments!' she boomed.

'Mask.'

'Mask.'

'Scissors.'

'Scissors.'

'Syringe.'

'Syringe.'

Minutes later Sally was in the garden, snipping the rose bushes with her

gardening scissors. Then she put on her mask and sprayed the bushes with her spray-pump. For forty-three whole minutes Sally was unaware of time. Then just at the end of the forty-third minute she heard a voice: 'How *can* you be bored on such a lovely morning?'

'Like this,' came a second voice.

'Yes, like this,' agreed a third.

The voices came from over the garden fence. Mrs Griptail was talking to her two children. Sally didn't often hear Mrs Griptail, for Mrs Griptail didn't often raise her voice. Sally peeped over the fence. She spied the two children, Morton and Mary, sitting on the back-door step, heads perched on paws, exactly like she herself had been sitting at the kitchen table.

'Why can't you find something to do, like me? I'm going to paint the front room today,' Mrs Griptail said.

'There's nothing to do,' Morton said.

'Except sit like this,' Mary said.

'Well, I don't want you disturbing me when I'm painting,' Mrs Griptail insisted. 'I'll be up a ladder. We don't want any accidents. Let's think of something for you to do so we can all be busy.'

They all thought.

'I know! You can play with Little Old Bear. What about that?' said Mrs Griptail.

'Oh yes, Mum!' Morton clapped his paws. 'I'd like to do that.'

'Yes, I'd like to do that,' Mary clapped her paws too.

'Well, we can't *both* do it,' said Morton.

'Oh yes, you can! You can share him.' Mrs Griptail quickly ran off to fetch Little Old Bear. Little Old Bear was the teddy she'd kept since she was a baby, and which always sat on her bedside table. 'Now, you will be careful with Little Old Bear, won't you? He's very old and very fragile.'

The children promised they would. But as soon as their mother had gone, they started tugging at the bear.

'I'll play with him first, then you play with him,' Mary said.

'And what am I supposed to do while you're playing with him?' Morton asked angrily.

'You can sit around being bored.'

'That's boring. I want to play with Little Old Bear all the time.' Morton pulled Little Old Bear from Mary's grasp.

'But Mum said we had to share him,' Mary cried.

'Right then,' Morton growled furiously. 'That's *exactly* what we'll do.'

He took hold of one of Little Old Bear's arms.

Pluck!

'One arm for you . . .'

Pluck!

'And one arm for me.'

'Morton!' cried Mary.

'One leg for you . . .'

Pluck!

'And one leg for me. And last of all . . .'

Rip!

'One head for you.'

'*Morton!*'

'And one body for me!'

After he'd finished, Morton cooled down a bit. He felt much better. Then he felt much worse. 'Oh dear, what have I done?'

'You've got us into a bucketful of trouble,' said

Mary miserably. 'That's what you've done. Mum'll be furious!'

'Oh, what are we going to do?' asked Morton.

'Yes, what are we going to do?' repeated Mary.

All this while, Surgeon Sally had been watching over the garden fence. When she saw the old teddy torn to pieces, her little eyes gleamed and her paws flexed itchily.

'Mary! Morton!' she called.

The children leapt up and immediately sat on the two piles of Little Old Bear so as to hide them.

They looked up guiltily. 'Hallo, Sally.'

'I think I might be able to help,' Surgeon Sally kindly offered. 'I'm a doctor, you know.'

Under Surgeon Sally's instructions, Mary and Morton picked up the pieces of Little Old Bear and, climbing over the fence, followed Sally through her garden and into her house. Soon, wearing masks, they were all gathered round the kitchen table.

'Head,' ordered Surgeon Sally.

'Head,' said Nurse Morton, handing Little Old Bear's head to Nurse Mary.

'Head,' echoed Mary, handing it on to Surgeon Sally.

The teddy's bits were neatly arranged on the white tablecloth, like pieces of a jigsaw puzzle. Morton and Mary were very excited about helping Sally. It was just like real doctors and nurses, especially as Sally *was* a real doctor. The operation was about to begin.

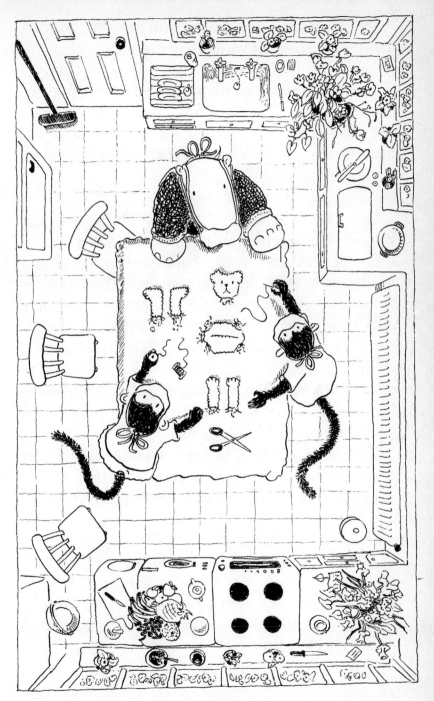

13

'Needle,' Surgeon Sally ordered.

'Needle,' said Morton, handing the needle to Mary.

'Needle,' said Mary, handing the needle to Surgeon Sally.

'Thread.'

'Thread.'

'Thread coming.'

All this time, Mrs Griptail had been busy painting. She hoped the children were still playing nicely. Although the front-room window was open she couldn't hear them. This worried her. They were so accident-prone, always leaping about, and she didn't want them ending up in Casualty. So she leaned forward a little, one leg on one ladder, a tail wrapped around the other . . .

In the kitchen, the operation on Little Old Bear was just beginning. Suddenly there came a terrifying shriek from over the garden wall.

Surgeon Sally looked up and listened for a moment. She whipped off her mask, rushed out of the kitchen, climbed the garden fence, and stuck her head through the open window of Mrs Griptail's front room.

'Don't move a muscle, Mrs Griptail,' Sally said. 'Leave everything to me. I'm a doctor, you know.'

Mrs Griptail was lying on the carpet with her left leg in an unusual position. Sally immediately climbed back over the fence into her kitchen and phoned for an ambulance. Then she turned to

Morton and Mary.

'We have an emergency. Nurse Mary, Nurse Morton: follow me!' Sally commanded.

Surgeon Sally, with the help of Morton and Mary, began to prepare Mrs Griptail for the journey to hospital. She made a splint from Morton's two drumsticks, and tied them round the patient's broken leg with old rags. Mary ran to fetch a bedspread from her bedroom, which she put over her mother to keep her warm, and Morton got a pillow from the sofa to put under her head. The two children were worried about their mother, but happy to be doing something helpful and not just playing at being doctors and nurses.

By the time the ambulance arrived, Mrs Griptail was all ready to go.

'So 'ow did it 'appen?' asked Ted when he saw the patient.

'Fell off a ladder, looks like,' said the other Ted.

'Fell off a ladder? Last one I'd expect to do that.'

'Shouldn't monkey about on ladders, that's what I say,' said Ted.

Mrs Griptail was carefully carried to the ambulance and lifted into the back. Surgeon Sally, Morton and Mary jumped in too, then the Teds sounded the siren. They swerved out into the street and raced towards Hilltop Hospital.

Surgeon Sally decided to set the leg herself. Two hours later, Dr Matthews, Nurse Kitty, Morton and Mary were gathered round Mrs Griptail's bed,

admiring the new white plaster-cast on her left leg.

'Sally's done a good job there,' beamed Dr
Matthews, adding, almost to himself, 'but then she
always does.'

'It will take some time to heal though,' Nurse
Kitty advised. 'You'll need to stay here for two
weeks, Mrs Griptail. But don't worry. I've arranged
for the children to stay with their Uncle Swing, as
you asked.'

'Oh, I will miss you both,' sighed Mrs Griptail.

'I'll miss you, Mum,' said Mary.

'And so will I,' chimed Morton.

'It would be nice to have something here to
remind me of you both and of home. I know! Little
Old Bear! I could put him just beside me on the
bedside table. Then when I wake up it'll be just like
waking up at home!'

The children looked at each other in guilty
silence. Just at that moment Surgeon Sally entered
the ward. She was holding something in her paws.

'Well, would you believe it!' exclaimed Mrs

Griptail. 'Here he is!'

Sally, without a word, handed Little Old Bear to Mrs Griptail. The astonished children peered closely at the bear but even they couldn't spot the fine stitching at the top of his arms and legs, and running all the way round his neck.

Later, Surgeon Sally marched into the staff room. Dr Matthews, delighted to see her on her day off, followed closely behind.

'Well Sally, I hope you didn't mind coming in today. But I know how you love your work. You were probably bored at home.'

'*Bored! Bored,* Dr Matthews?' she bellowed. 'I haven't had time to be *bored.* I've been busy operating non-stop since the very crack of dawn!'

DR MATTHEWS IS TAKEN ILL

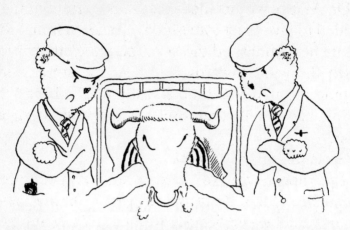

It had been one of those days at Hilltop Hospital.
The two Teds had been delivering patients to
Casualty all morning, like milkmen delivering
bottles. Dr Matthews had been running up and
down the wards, ears flapping, stethoscope flying. It
was the last patient of the morning, an enormous
bull called Jerzy, who caused the accident.

He entered the ward, tossing and turning on the
trolley. And as he was lifted from the trolley to the
bed, he bellowed dangerously.

'What's all this noise?' Dr Matthews growled.

'E's been like this since we got 'im in the
ambulance. Can't you give 'im something to quieten
'im down?' said Ted.

'Yer, like a muzzle,' said the other Ted.

'Or a mallet,' said Ted.

Jerzy bellowed again, swishing his horns from side
to side and knocking over the side table.

''Elp!' cried Ted.

'Yer, 'elp!' cried Ted.

Dr Matthews decided the Teds were right: he needed to give Jerzy something to quieten him down before he demolished the hospital. Dr Matthews ran down the ward towards the medicine store-room, leaping through the double swing doors. If only he hadn't had a tail, everything would have been all right.

'Aaaahhhrrr!' he howled.

The howl was so loud even Jerzy stopped bellowing. Nurse Kitty ran to where Dr Matthews lay and knelt down beside him. 'Poor Dr Matthews! Now, do lie still so I can have a look at it.'

'I'm perfectly all right,' Dr Matthews insisted, and howled again.

'I won't hurt you. Now, I'm just going to apply a little pressure – '

'Aaaahhhrrr!' Then Dr Matthews barked, 'I told you, Kitty, there's nothing the matter with me. Look, I can wag my tail without any problem.'

He wagged it once and howled in pain again.

'What's all this noise?' boomed a voice from the corridor. It was Surgeon Sally. When she saw the doctor lying on the floor, she immediately bent down and swiftly inspected his swollen tail. Dr Matthews remained perfectly silent.

'Looks like a broken tail-bone. Nurse Kitty, prepare a bed. Teds, bring over a stretcher. We've got a new patient.'

'Nurse! Nurse!'

Kitty knew it was Dr Matthews calling from his bed. He had been calling every half hour. First he wanted a glass of water, then he wanted ice in the water, then he wanted a slice of lemon in the water, and then he drank the water and needed to go to the lavatory.

'*And* he refuses to take any medicine,' Kitty sighed. She was down in the dispensary with Clare and Arthur, the lab mice.

'You would've thought Dr Matthews would know better,' Arthur commented.

'I was wondering if you could mix the medicine up with something to make it taste nicer,' suggested Nurse Kitty.

'We're chemists, not chefs. We're very busy chemists, too,' squeaked Arthur.

'Hmmm.' Clare looked along the shelves of glass jars and bottles filled with orange, blue and green liquids. 'I think I might be able to help, Kitty.'

★ ★ ★

20

'Nurse! Nurse!' growled Dr Matthews.

He sat miserably in his untidy bed. Over the bedcover, the bedside table and the floor were books from Mrs Bifocal's mobile hospital library, none of them touched. Dr Matthews was so bored he kept taking his own pulse and temperature. He listened to his heart with his stethoscope. Then he put the stethoscope up to the radio, and to the daffodils his friends had brought him. Then he growled again, 'Nurse! Nurse!'

'What is it now?' said Nurse Kitty, as she entered the ward with Clare, who was holding a bottle and teaspoon.

'I've taken my temperature and my pulse and they're normal. I'm cured.'

'But can you wag your tail?'

'I don't *need* to wag my tail. I'm not in the mood to wag my tail.'

Nurse Kitty didn't want to be strict with Dr Matthews but she knew she had to be, for his own good. 'You're not cured until Surgeon Sally says you are. Those are my instructions, Dr Matthews. Now it's time for your medicine.'

'I'm not going to take my medicine. It tastes horrible.'

'Don't worry, Dr Matthews,' Clare squeaked happily. 'I've put something in the medicine to make it taste nice.'

'I don't care *what* you've put in it. I'm not taking it.'

'You'll like it, Dr Matthews. It's braised bone and biscuit flavour.'

Dr Matthews's nose twitched.

'Braised bone?'

'Mmm.' Clare tipped some mixture on to the spoon.

'What sort of biscuits?'

'I'm not sure,' said Clare, holding out the spoon. 'You'll have to try.'

Dr Matthews sniffed the teaspoon carefully, then licked it clean. After a moment he asked for more.

'In an hour's time,' Nurse Kitty replied firmly, 'if you're good.'

Later, in the staff room, Kitty asked Clare what she'd added to the medicine.

'Nothing,' giggled Clare. 'Nothing at all.'

The quietest time of day in the hospital ward is early afternoon, after lunch and before visiting hours. It was summer, and the sun filtered through the windows. The patients were dozing; the nurses were chatting, checking medicine charts and making tea in the staff room. This was when Dr Matthews chose to creep out of bed. He slipped his white coat over his pyjamas and stepped lightly out of the ward into the corridor.

'Ah, Matthews!' The voice came from right behind him.

Dr Matthews prepared to run, but turning round saw it was only Dr Atticus. 'I wondered,' Dr Atticus yawned, 'if you'd give me a paw. Problem with a troublesome patient.'

Dr Atticus was so dozy he hadn't even heard about Dr Matthews's injury.

'Troublesome patient, eh?' Dr Matthews shook his head. 'Nothing worse.'

'You're telling me. First he makes all this noise in the ward, then he keeps calling for nurses, and now he won't take his medicine.'

'Won't take his medicine? Sounds like Jerzy, the patient I admitted this morning,' Dr Matthews scowled. 'Well, I'll soon see about him.'

Dr Matthews followed Dr Atticus to the ward where Jerzy sat in bed, looking very cross.

'You're not the only patient in this hospital,' Dr Matthews began. 'We haven't got all day to wait while you decide whether or not to take your medicine.'

'You don't need to wait,' Jerzy snorted. 'I can tell you now I'm not going to take it.'

'You're not, eh?' Then Dr Matthews suddenly had an idea. 'Not even if it's been flavoured with fresh spring grass?'

'No.' Jerzy tossed his horns. 'Fresh grass, did you say?'

'That's right,' said Dr Matthews.

'With morning dew on it?'

'I'm not sure about that. You'll have to try it.'

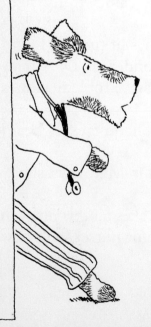

So Jerzy tried the medicine and even licked his lips after. Of course it hadn't really been flavoured with fresh spring grass. Dr Matthews had made that up, but Jerzy believed him so completely he really did think he could taste fresh spring grass. Dr Matthews smiled at his own cleverness.

24

'And now there's just your injection,' said Dr Atticus, holding up a syringe with a fine needle.

'NO WAY!' bellowed Jerzy. Instantly, he was out of bed and charging down the ward. Dr Atticus stood dozily watching Jerzy escape, but Dr Matthews sprang after him. Jerzy disappeared through the swing doors. Dr Matthews dashed through the swing doors too. If only he hadn't had a tail everything would have been all right.

'Aaaahhhrrr!' he howled.

'And this time,' Surgeon Sally ordered, 'you'll stay in bed until *I* say you're ready to leave it.'

'Yes, Sally. Sorry, Sally,' nodded Dr Matthews.

'You're not the only patient in this hospital, you know. I haven't got all day to attend to you when you decide to go for a walk before you're better.'

'Yes, Sally. Sorry, Sally.'

After seeing all the trouble he'd caused, Dr Matthews had become the perfect patient. He quietly read the books from Mrs Bifocal's library, listened to the radio, took his medicine and hardly ever called out for a nurse.

Later that afternoon Nurse Kitty dropped by with a visitor. Jerzy was now better and had come to apologise. He'd brought a box of biscuits.

'But before Dr Matthews has any biscuits he must have his medicine,' Nurse Kitty insisted with a smile.

Dr Matthews took the medicine without a murmur or a growl.

'Ah,' Jerzy beamed, 'I wish I'd been able to behave like that. The perfect patient, isn't he, Nurse Kitty?'

'Oh yes,' said Nurse Kitty. 'But then Dr Matthews is a doctor, so he ought to know how to behave. Isn't that right, Dr Matthews?'

'If you say so, Kitty,' Dr Matthews replied sheepishly.

'And now,' Kitty continued, 'there's only your injection, Dr Matthews.'

'Injection?'

'Mmm.' Nurse Kitty knew how much Dr Matthews hated injections. In fact, she could see him preparing to leap out of bed, so she added, 'Now you'll see, Jerzy, what little fuss Dr Matthews makes about having an injection. Oh yes, a real lesson for us all.'

Dr Matthews looked helplessly at the syringe in Nurse Kitty's paw.

'Now, just turn over, Dr Matthews. That's it . . . Ready? It's not going to hurt – one – little – bit.'

THE BLOOD BANK

'Night-shifts. I 'ate night-shifts,' said Ted.

'You 'ate day-shifts,' said the other Ted.

'I 'ate day-shifts. But I *really* 'ate night-shifts. I should be in bed.'

The ambulance halted and the two Teds stepped out into the quiet street. They rang the bell of a small house. Ruby came to the door. She looked extremely pale – especially for a vampire bat. Ruby explained that, due to a chill she had caught, she hadn't been able to get out and about of an evening. This meant she hadn't been getting enough to eat, or, more importantly, to drink.

Within minutes Ruby was safely tucked away in the back of the ambulance as it hurtled down the darkened street, speeding towards Hilltop Hospital.

'I mean, if people were a little more considerate and didn't get ill at night, it'd make our job a lot easier, wouldn't it?' continued Ted.

'Well, if people were a little more considerate they wouldn't get ill in the day neither. That'd make our job a lot easier,' said Ted.

'That's right.'

'Although, come to think of it, we wouldn't 'ave a job then, would we?'

They reached the hill. Above them the ward night-lights gave out a green glow from the hospital windows. Just then the ambulance stopped.

'Why're you stopping?' asked Ted. 'This is an emergency.'

'I 'aven't stopped. The ambulance 'as.'

Ted tried to start the engine, but nothing happened. The ambulance stood silently in the cold night.

'Better get out and check the engine,' said Ted.

'*I'm* not getting out to check the engine. It's freezing out there,' the other Ted replied.

'Well, it's no use *me* getting out. I don't know anything about engines.'

'Well, as a matter of fact, neither do I.' Ted picked up the radio receiver and called for help.

It was quiet at Hilltop Hospital. The night staff of moles, foxes, cats and bats were whispering softly to each other at

the end of the wards, and drinking tea under the warm, soft lights. Dr Matthews was on duty. He and Nurse Kitty were sitting in the staff room when Ted's emergency call came through.

Dr Matthews knew it was important to get Ruby to the hospital as soon as possible. He thought for a while, and decided on the quickest way to transport her there. Then he told the Teds.

'I really, really 'ate night-shifts,' said Ted furiously, as the two trudged up the hill carrying Ruby on a stretcher. 'This is unbearable – the last straw. As soon as we get to the 'ospital, I'm telling that Dr Matthews I'm leaving. That's final.'

The other Ted had often heard Ted say he was leaving his job. This time Ted seemed to mean it. He looked down at Ruby, wrapped in two blankets. She looked paler than the white pillow beneath her.

At last they reached the hospital. Dr Matthews and Nurse Kitty were waiting anxiously right by the doors. The Teds transferred Ruby on to the trolley and wheeled her to Casualty.

'Can I 'ave a word with you, Dr Matthews?' said Ted.

'Can it wait, Ted?'

Before Ted could reply, Dr Matthews had disappeared into the ward.

Dr Matthews had immediately noticed how pale

Ruby looked. Straight away, he rang the lab. Down in the lab was the blood bank.

The blood bank was a large fridge, so large it was a whole room. In the room were rows and rows of bottles, like little milk bottles, except that each one was filled with blood. Clare and Arthur, the lab mice, looked after the blood. They also collected it: every Tuesday they ran the blood clinic. Animals from the town who volunteered to give blood came to the hospital and sat in the waiting room until the lab mice called them one at a time into the surgery. There, Clare and Arthur would roll up the patient's sleeve and carefully remove some of his or her blood with a syringe. Afterwards, the patient would lie down for a few minutes; a nurse would bring over a cup of tea and one of Arthur's scrumptious home-made chocolate biscuits. It was a regular little tea party.

The hospital always needed blood. There was never enough.

When they got Dr Matthews's call, Clare and Arthur knew the first thing they had to do was check Ruby's blood type. They hurried up to Casualty with a syringe.

'You can't just *leave*.' Nurse Kitty watched Ted empty his locker of ancient honey jars and spare cap badges.

'I've 'ad enough,' Ted said.

''E's 'ad enough,' said the other Ted. ''E 'ates night-shifts, you see.'

'I 'ate day-shifts. But I *really* 'ate night-shifts.'

'Yes, but the hospital can't just close at the end of the *day*, Ted,' Kitty insisted. 'A hospital never stops.'

The phone rang.

''Allo?' growled Ted.

'It's Matthews. Is Nurse Kitty there?'

'Ah, Dr Matthews. Can I 'ave a word with you?'

'Can it wait, Ted?' Dr Matthews hurried on. 'We've got an emergency on our paws. Tell Nurse Kitty to go down to the lab immediately.'

On the lab table was a test-tube of Ruby's blood.

'AB negative,' Arthur squeaked miserably.

'That's rare, isn't it?' Nurse Kitty asked.

'Rare isn't the word. We haven't got any of this type in our whole blood bank. It's hopeless, hopeless, hopeless.'

'Gosh,' Nurse Kitty exclaimed, looking through the glass door of the blood bank, 'all that blood and not a drop we can use.'

'We've tried nearby hospitals but they haven't got any either,' said Arthur.

'What're we going to do?' Nurse Kitty asked.

'There's nothing we can do,' Arthur squeaked in despair. 'It's hopeless, hopeless, hopeless. Ruby must be given the right type of blood and we just haven't got any.'

All this time, Clare had been sitting on the lab table, stroking her whiskers thoughtfully. 'We *might* have some,' she piped up. 'What I mean is, one of us might have the right blood.'

'Us?' Dr Matthews asked.

'Yes. You might have it. Or you, Kitty. Or you, Arthur. Let's find out!'

Clare jumped off the desk and got out the syringes. Everyone took it in turn to have a sample of their blood taken. It was just like the Tuesday blood clinic except there were no chocolate biscuits.

'Do you think this is a good idea?' Dr Matthews asked, mainly because he hated having injections.

'It's Ruby's only chance,' Clare reminded him.

Fortunately, Clare was so expert with needles that even Dr Matthews admitted it didn't hurt.

Clare then took Arthur's blood and he took hers.

Soon all the blood was tested.

'Hopeless, hopeless, hopeless.' Arthur's tail sank. 'None of it is AB negative.'

'What about the Teds?' asked Clare.

'It's pointless,' said Arthur, 'a chance in a million.'

'We mustn't give up hope,' Claire said firmly.

She rang the Teds' office.

'There's as much chance of them having the right blood as there is we'll have a heat wave tomorrow,' declared Arthur.

'AB negative!' squealed Clare.

Arthur couldn't believe it, but there it was – just what Ruby needed. Immediately, Ted was asked to sit down while Clare took some more blood from him. Ted didn't mind, as he was promised one of Arthur's home-made biscuits.

As soon as they had the blood, Kitty, Dr Matthews, Clare and Arthur raced up to Casualty and set up the drip by Ruby's bed. But then Arthur thought of some more bad news.

'We're going to need more blood. And we can't take any more from Ted.'

'What about the other Ted?' Dr Matthews suggested.

'Hopeless, hopeless, hopeless.

34

There's as much chance of the other Ted having the right blood type as there is we'll have a heat wave tomorrow.'

'But they're brothers,' Kitty told him.

'Doesn't make any difference,' said Arthur, shaking his head. 'Just because they're brothers doesn't mean they'll have the same blood type.'

'But they're twins,' Kitty reminded him.

'Doesn't make any difference. Just because they're twins doesn't mean they'll have the same blood type.'

'But they're *identical* twins!' Clare squeaked.

'Doesn't – ' Arthur turned to Clare. 'Are they?'

'Yes.'

Arthur turned to Dr Matthews. 'Where is the other Ted?'

'No way!' said the other Ted.

They'd found him by the front doors of the hospital, holding a bag of his belongings. He was about to step out into the frosty night, determined never to set foot in Hilltop again, except possibly as a patient.

'First you make me do day-shifts – and I 'ate day-shifts – and *then* you make me do night-shifts – and I *really* 'ate night-shifts. And now you even want my blood. This really takes the biscuit.'

Dr Matthews listened to Ted's complaints, realising he hadn't always valued Ted's work as much as he should have done. But at that moment his main concern was his patient.

'It's Ruby's last chance, Ted,' said Dr Matthews.

Ted stood in silence, one paw gripping his bag, the other holding the door-handle. With an angry scowl on his face, he put the bag down.

'It'd better not 'urt,' he growled. 'And I want *two* of Arthur's special 'ome-made scrumptious chocolate biscuits afterwards.'

The next morning, the sun, unusually bright for winter, lay level with the windows and filled the ward with buttery light.

'Look at the beautiful day,' Nurse Kitty purred.

'Mmm. We might even have a heat wave,' Dr Matthews commented.

Just as he spoke the two Teds entered the ward: one of them wanted a word. As they both approached Dr Matthews they suddenly saw Ruby. Breakfast had just been sent up, and Ruby was tucking into a plate of grilled tomatoes. They were amazed to see her looking so well, so happy, and so rosy.

'Ah, Ted,' Dr Matthews smiled. 'You wanted a word.'

'Er . . . that's right, Dr Matthews.' Ted had definitely decided to leave Hilltop: he'd spent all night preparing what he was going to say. But now, seeing Ruby, he somehow felt different. 'Well, I did 'ave something to say . . . I was going to say I was leaving. But I realise now 'ow much this 'ospital needs me.'

'Yer, 'e realises 'ow much this 'ospital needs 'im,'

said the other Ted.

'This place would fall apart without me.'

'Yer, it'd fall apart without 'im.'

'So I'm stayin'. That's what I wanted to say.'

'Yer, 'e's stayin'. That's what 'e wanted to say.'

'That's wonderful.' Dr Matthews and Nurse Kitty smiled. They thanked the Teds for all their hard work, admitting how often they forgot to praise them.

'It's funny though,' Dr Matthews added. 'It never occurred to me before you were identical twins.'

'Didn't it?' said the two Teds together.

'No.'

'It just goes to show you don't know much about us, Dr Matthews,' said the two Teds together again.

Just before they left, Dr Matthews said, 'And thanks again, Ted, for deciding not to leave us.'

'*Me*? Leave 'Illtop 'Ospital? No way. I wouldn't dream of leaving. No, you must mean my brother 'ere.'

'*Me*? Leave 'Illtop 'Ospital?' said the other Ted. 'No way. I wouldn't dream of leaving. No, you must mean my brother 'ere.'

Dr Matthews looked from one Ted to the other. The Teds both smiled back with identical grins on their faces.

RAG WEEK AT HILLTOP HOSPITAL

Every summer there was a Rag Week at Hilltop Hospital.

It was a week of jokes and fun to raise money for heart research, to help patients like Dandy Lyon. Dandy had been at Hilltop for a long, long time, waiting for a new heart. In fact he had been waiting for so long, he was beginning to, well, lose heart.

'Now don't you worry, Dandy,' purred Staff Nurse Kitty, tucking him up in bed the day before Rag Week began. 'It won't be long now.'

The same afternoon all the hospital staff gathered for a final meeting to organise the week ahead. Nurse Kitty was planning the raffle. Surgeon Sally, who was good at sewing, had made beautiful rag-dolls to sell. Dr Matthews had put together a Rag Mag which was full of jokes like, 'What do you give a pig with a sore snout? – Oinkment.' And the lab mice, Clare and Arthur, were going to dress up as doctors and push a hospital bed round the town, collecting money in a bucket.

All the hospital staff were taking part, except Dr Atticus, the anaesthetist, who was too lazy.

'You must be the laziest doctor in the world,' Arthur said.

'I can't help that,' Dr Atticus yawned. 'That's how I am.'

That was always his answer, but this year Clare had an idea.

'You could help Arthur and me . . .'

'You mean, push a bed round along the streets? I don't know about that.' Just the thought made Dr Atticus feel tired.

'But Dr Atticus, just think of poor Dandy Lyon. He's the sort of patient this Rag Week is for. Besides, you don't have to push the bed along the street. You could be *in* the bed. You could be the pretend patient.'

'Oh, I see.' Dr Atticus brightened up a bit at this.

'You just have to wear pyjamas,' Clare said, trying to tempt him.

Dr Atticus then actually had an idea. 'What time would we start in the morning?'

'Whenever you're ready, Dr Atticus,' said Clare.

'Well, why don't you wheel the bed round to my house at about ten, hmmm?'

So they did. Dr Atticus set his alarm for 9.55 am; he was just about awake when the doorbell rang. He got out of bed and, still in his pink pyjamas, walked to the front door, and then straight into the hospital bed waiting for him on the pavement. He hardly had to open his eyes.

'Morning, Dr Atticus,' Clare piped.

'Morning, Atticus,' Arthur added.

There was no answer. Dr Atticus was asleep.

Deep in his shell he slept the whole morning. Even though cars hooted, even though passers-by laughed as Clare and Arthur pushed him through the streets and the shopping centre, even though coins clanged in the bucket tied to the end of the bed, Dr Atticus didn't wake up once. Only at one o'clock sharp did his head pop out from his shell, like a cuckoo from a clock.

'Must be lunch time,' he yawned.

Clare and Arthur had stopped at Hilltop Tavern, halfway up the hill to the hospital.

'I don't mind keeping guard of the bed,' Dr Atticus volunteered, 'while you two go and have some lunch.'

'That's very thoughtful of you, Dr Atticus,' Clare smiled. 'Arthur and I are quite exhausted.'

'Not at all.' He added, 'So um . . . if you'll just bring out a tray of food for me, I'll be quite happy here.'

'That Atticus! I've heard of breakfast in bed but really . . .' grumbled Arthur as they entered the tavern and ordered Dr Atticus's lunch.

Dr Atticus stayed awake long enough to enjoy his lettuce salad in the afternoon sunlight. The meal, however, made him a little dozy, and he soon found his head sinking down into his shell again. The last thing he remembered was the meal tray slipping off the bed. It clanged against something made of metal. He was too sleepy to wonder what the metal thing was. Later he realised it must have been the hospital bed's brake-lever.

At Hilltop Hospital, Nurse Kitty was about to begin the raffle. Surgeon Sally was selling her dolls and Dr Matthews had just read a joke from his Rag Mag to the patients' visitors in the main ward. As he stood waiting for them to laugh, the wall-phone rang.

'Matthews here,' he answered.

It was a message to say a new heart for Dandy Lyon had just been found. The two Teds were ordered to collect it at once. Dr Matthews quickly informed Surgeon Sally.

'Prepare the theatre, Kitty!' she boomed.

Rag week, for the moment, was postponed.

The bed rolled slowly at first, but it was a steep hill and the wheels were well oiled. Dr Atticus was dreaming he was swimming smoothly underwater.

As the bed picked up speed, it set a straight course towards a church. Just in front of the silent, tranquil building was a silent, tranquil lake. The bed bumped and bounced across the grass, then flipped and dipped and disappeared into the water. It was the sound of quacking ducks that made the five nuns quickly finish their prayers and rush out to the lakeside.

They were just in time to see a figure climbing on to the bank. When they saw he was wearing pink pyjamas they phoned the police.

Police Sergeant Gristle, an old boxer, arrived within minutes.

'But I'm a doctor, I tell you,' Dr Atticus kept insisting.

'If you're a doctor, why're you wearing pyjamas?' argued the Sergeant. 'Doctors wear white coats and carry stethoscopes. Only patients wear pyjamas.'

'But I'm a doctor *pretending* to be a patient.'

'You're just wasting my time. Before I take you in, I've got to clear the street. In a few moments an ambulance is coming this way – with a very important organ in it. For a very important operation.'

Dr Atticus immediately guessed what that organ was.

'But I'm the anaesthetist. They can't start the operation without me. You must let me go.'

'Sorry mate,' said the Sergeant, 'you're coming with me.'

Dr Atticus sat miserably on the solid mattress of his cell-bed. If he didn't get to the hospital in time, Dandy Lyon wouldn't be able to get his new heart. All because of my laziness, he thought guiltily.

But I can't help it, he reminded himself. That's how I am.

This time reminding himself didn't help. In fact, it only made him more miserable, and thinking of poor Dandy Lyon without a new heart made him feel quite ill. His stomach and head began to ache. He lay down on the hard bed, but the pain became so great he couldn't even sleep. He began to moan.

'What is it?' asked the Sergeant when he heard the noise.

'Is there . . . is there a doctor in the house?' Dr Atticus gasped as his head sunk very slowly into his shell.

Meanwhile, in the operating theatre, under bright yellow spotlights, the surgical team were gathered round DandyLyon.

'Will I be all right?' he asked.

'Of course you will,' promised Nurse Kitty. 'Cross my heart.'

'Sterilize instruments,' Surgeon Sally ordered.

'Instruments sterilized.'

'Scalpel.'

'Scalpel.'

'Anaesthetic.'

'No anaesthetic.'

'*No anaesthetic?*' Surgeon Sally looked up.

'Dr Atticus isn't here yet,' Dr Matthews commented. 'We'll just have to wait.'

When the two Teds received an emergency call from the police station, they didn't realise they were being summoned to collect Dr Atticus. Even when they came face to face with their patient they didn't realise; partly because Dr Atticus had his head buried in his shell, partly because he was wearing pink pyjamas, and partly because he was moaning.

'What's the matter with 'im?' Ted asked the Sergeant.

'How should *I* know?' barked the Sergeant. 'I'm only a policeman.'

Dr Atticus felt himself being lifted on to the stretcher and then being put into the ambulance. As he heard the ambulance doors swing shut, he thought how strange it was that he had begun the day pretending to be a patient, and now he *was* a patient. Dr Atticus began to wonder if, in the same

45

way, he'd become a slow and lazy tortoise because he thought that's how tortoises always were. With the sirens sounding, the ambulance raced towards Hilltop Hospital. And now Dandy Lyon's life was at stake. So then Dr Atticus wondered if he could change himself by *thinking* he was different. What if he saw himself as bright and alert and full of energy, like Clare, the lab mouse, for instance?

He thought he would try it out. And just as he had decided this, his stomach and his head began to feel much better.

In the theatre, the surgical team were growing more and more impatient. Surgeon Sally said, 'That Dr Atticus! He'd be late for an operation even if he was the patient.'

'He can't help it,' Nurse Kitty said. 'It's just how he is.'

At that moment they heard the ambulance screech to a halt outside.

The two Teds ran to the back of the ambulance to open the doors. Just as they turned the handles the doors burst open, knocking them both to the ground. Out dashed a tortoise in pink pyjamas. Before they could get up, the patient had leapt towards the entrance of the hospital and disappeared inside.

'Well, blow me! Did you see 'im'? It was Dr Atticus!' said Ted.

'Don't be stupid. Course it wasn't Dr Atticus! 'E couldn't run like that. Besides, 'e was wearing pink

46

pyjamas,' said the other Ted.

Dr Atticus dashed into the staff room to grab a white coat and a stethoscope. Two nurses looked up from their magazines to see a white-coated figure disappearing down the corridor.

'That was Dr Atticus, wasn't it?'

'Naaaaa. Couldn't have been.'

OPERATION IN PROGRESS

The theatre doors crashed open and a doctor in a white coat and mask rushed in.

'Well,' said the figure, standing in the yellow light over the operating table, 'let's get on with it. We haven't got all day. Get that heart out of the fridge please, Nurse Kitty. Matthews, hand me the anaesthetic. Sally, let me know when you're ready.'

Sally looked at the masked figure in amazement.

'Who are you?' she demanded.

'Who do you think I am? I'm Dr Atticus, of course. And I've a patient to see to.'

But this wasn't the Atticus they knew. Within seconds he had prepared the staff to operate.

It was left to Sally to say the final words. 'Check anaesthetic.'

'Anaesthetic already checked!' beamed Dr Atticus.

'Administer anaesthetic.'

'Administering anaesthetic!' Dr Atticus declared with zest. 'Anaesthetic administered!'

The operation began.

It was Friday, the last day of Rag Week. Dr Matthews still had eight copies of his Rag Mag to sell. That afternoon, in the ward, he was reading a joke from his magazine to four visitors, who were gathered around Dandy Lyon's bed. The operation had been a success, and Dandy had been laughing and chatting and singing all week. He seemed to laugh at almost anything. Nevertheless, Dr Matthews was still waiting for Dandy, as well as the four visitors, to laugh at his joke when Dr Atticus stepped into the ward.

'Let me have a go, Matthews.' He plucked the magazine from Dr Matthews's paws.

'*You?* You'll put them to sleep,' Dr Matthews said unkindly.

But Dr Atticus read out a joke with such sparkle, such verve, that the visitors immediately burst out laughing. They all bought two copies of the Rag Mag each.

'How did you do that?' Dr Matthews asked.

'It's the way I tell 'em,' smiled Dr Atticus.

'I wish I could tell them like that.'

'Wish hard then,' was Dr Atticus's advice, 'and it might happen. Still, I can't stand here all day telling jokes. I must run.'

And, to Dr Matthews's surprise, he did.

OLD GRACEY GREYSHELL'S
LAST DAY

Sometimes, when Staff Nurse Kitty was very busy walking up and down the ward, taking a temperature here, delivering a bed-pan there, she wondered if she wouldn't rather be a patient. They looked so comfortable and relaxed in the bright sunlit ward: Harvey Blacksmith, the horse, reading a horror book called *Nightmare,* Flora Nightingale listening to opera on her Walkman, and Sigmund, the fruit bat, pouring himself a glass of orange juice. Only Gracey Greyshell didn't look relaxed or happy.

Gracey Greyshell was one hundred and forty years old. That was old, even for a turtle. Nurse Kitty did all she could to make Gracey comfortable but the more trouble she took, the more miserable Gracey became.

'I don't understand why Gracey's so sad,'

Kitty confided in Dr Matthews. 'I'd be really happy to lie in bed all day and be served breakfast, lunch and dinner.'

'Well, Kitty, not much chance of that today. Three emergency cases have just arrived in Ward Ten. We need all the spare staff we can lay our paws on.'

Nurse Kitty was already very tired from the morning ward round, but she accepted the news without complaint. Soon she and most of her staff were following Dr Matthews to Ward Ten.

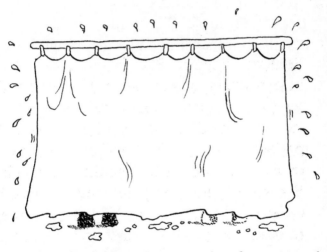

When they had gone, it was quiet, for a very short while, in the main ward. There were two nurses left on duty. They decided to make the most of the few minutes' peace to give Rachel, the rhino, who was suffering from a skin complaint, a bed-bath. They fetched a bowl of warm water and some soap. Soon, from behind the curtain drawn round the bed, the splashing of water and the rasping of sponges across hide could be heard.

It's a strange fact that as soon as nurses are busy, patients cry out, one by one, 'Nurse! Nurse!' The first was Sigmund, the bat.

'Nurse! Nurse!' he squeaked.

'Won't be long!' one of nurses called above the sound of splashing and squelching.

Sigmund's cries woke up Gracey Greyshell. She was surprised to see no nurse on the ward. Without further thought, she lowered herself out of bed, slipped on her dressing-gown and slippers, and tottered over to Sigmund's bed.

'What's the trouble, Sigmund?'

'Oh, hallo, Gracey. I need some orange juice. I'm parched.'

'Give me the jug, then.'

Gracey had been in hospital for so long she knew just where the ward kitchen was and where in the fridge the orange juice was kept.

'Thanks, Gracey. You've even put some ice in it!' said Sigmund when she returned. He was delighted. 'What a life-saver you are. I would've died without a drink.'

'You wouldn't have died, Sigmund,' Gracey corrected him, 'but I'm glad I could help.'

'Nurse! Nurse!' came a weak, chirrupy voice from further down the ward.

'We'll be with you in a moment!' the two nurses called out. Rachel's bath was taking them longer than they'd thought. There seemed to be a lot of skin to wash.

'Can I help, Flora?' Gracey stood by Flora's bed.

'Oh Gracey! The batteries have run out in my Walkman. It's unbearable! I'm *so* miserable without my music!'

'Well, there's not much I can do about that.'

'But I *must* have music, Gracey. And I can't sing because of my throat problem.' Flora looked crestfallen.

Gracey sat down at her bedside and thought back to some of the songs she used to sing when she was a little turtle. They were sea shanties mostly. Gracey had a good memory, which was fortunate as she hadn't sung those songs for a hundred and thirty years. She began to sing them now. She didn't have the clear, bell-like voice of Flora Nightingale. It was quivery and fragile, like most elderly voices, but somehow this made the old songs sound even sweeter. The thin notes fluttered like sparrows from bed to bed all the way down the ward. By the time

she'd finished, everyone was listening and everyone clapped.

'Oh, thank you, thank you, Gracey,' Flora trilled. 'I feel *so* much better. I would've simply died without some music.'

'You wouldn't have died, Flora,' Gracey corrected her, 'but I'm glad I could help.'

'Nurse! Nurse!' came a neigh from further down the ward.

'We're nearly done!' the two nurses called out, just as they turned Rachel on her front and found lots more skin to wash on her back.

'What's the matter, dear?' asked Gracey, as she made her way over to Harvey Blacksmith. He put down his book *Nightmare* and took off his glasses.

'I'm living in terror,' he whispered, hoarsely.

'Why's that, dear?'

'I'm going to have . . . an operation.'

'I know you're going to have an operation. But there's no need to be terrified about *that*.'

Gracey then explained patiently how, over many years – 'and I mean *many* years' – she'd known lots of others who'd had operations, and they had all got better in the end.

'Oh, thank you, Gracey. Listening to you has made me feel much happier. I really thought I was going to die with worry.'

'You wouldn't have died, Harvey,' Gracey corrected him, 'but I'm glad I could help. Oh, there's one other thing you could do to stop being terrified.'

'Yes?'

'Read something else.'

'Nurse! Nurse!' cried all the patients in the ward.

'Almost finished!' the two nurses called out, just as they reached Rachel's toes – and discovered her toe-nails could do with a clipping.

'What do you all want now?' Gracey laughed.

'Our morning coffee, of course,' the patients complained.

Every morning at 11.00 am sharp, Mrs Fielding, a country mouse, entered the ward with her squeaky-wheeled tea-trolley. It was 11.05 am and the ward was squeakless.

Mrs Fielding must be ill, thought Gracey. Immediately she trotted into the kitchen where the trolley was kept. At 11.10 am the patients heard the familiar squeak at the end of the ward and they all cheered.

'We're dying for a cuppa!' they cried.

The emergencies in Ward Ten kept Nurse Kitty and her staff on their hind-legs until supper-time. So Gracey found herself helping to serve lunch and afternoon tea, as well as singing a few more songs for Flora Nightingale. By the time Kitty had returned to the ward, Gracey had only just got back into bed. Both were exhausted, but only one was happy.

In fact, Kitty was so surprised to see Gracey sitting up in bed smiling that she asked Gracey if she was all right.

'Oh yes. But what about you?'

'Oh!' Kitty whined. 'It's been go, go, go all day long!'

'It's been like that here,' Gracey nodded. 'It's been wonderful.'

But Kitty didn't understand what she meant until later.

After supper Gracey lay in bed and watched the sun setting. It was like a huge apricot held in the blue sky. As she felt its warmth, an answering glow came from inside her. It was the feeling she had always had – although not for a long time – at the end of a good day's work. The years of her working life, all one hundred of them, came back to her. Gracey was never happier than when she was busy, and felt little pleasure if she couldn't be of some use. So, with happy memories in her mind, she watched the sun. And as she watched, it seemed to grow bigger and

bigger until she felt as though she were flying right into it. The warmth made her sleepy. In the end she couldn't stay awake any longer.

When the patients woke up the next morning they saw that Gracey's bed was empty. Nurse Kitty was emptying Gracey's bedside cupboard. They asked where she was, so Kitty told them.

'She *was* one hundred and forty,' Kitty explained. 'She had a long life. And a happy one, I think. In fact, I had never seen her happier than she looked yesterday evening.'

It was then that Sigmund told Kitty how Gracey had brought him his orange juice, Flora described how Gracey had sung sea shanties to her, and Harvey told how Gracey had reassured him about his operation. Then the other patients chatted about Gracey bringing them morning coffee.

All this surprised Kitty. Just at that moment, as she cleared out some papers from the bedside drawer, a few old black-and-white photos spilt on to the bed. As she picked them up, Kitty saw they were photos of Gracey; a much younger Gracey. And in some of them she wore a Staff Nurse's uniform.

Kitty looked very thoughtful.

When Dr Matthews came by later to do the morning ward round he commented, 'Sorry about the extra work in Ward Ten, Kitty. Especially after what you said about wanting to lie in bed all day.'

'Lie in bed? Me?' Kitty said quickly. 'Oh, don't apologise, Dr Matthews. I should be only too grateful there's work to do. After all, that's why I became a nurse. Oh no, I'd be bored to death lying in a bed all day!'

HAPPY CHRISTMAS, DR MATTHEWS

Christmas at Hilltop Hospital was usually a happy time for Dr Matthews, but not this year. Dr Bickerbeak had joined the staff.

Dr Bickerbeak was a tall, thin bird with alert, beady eyes behind wire-framed glasses. He wore a white coat which was immaculately white, with all the buttons on it.

Dr Matthews also wore a white coat, but sometimes it had spots of blood on a sleeve, or biscuit crumbs down a lapel, and Nurse Kitty noticed there was always at least one button missing.

Right from the beginning, Dr Bickerbeak and Dr Matthews didn't get on.

'It's against the rules, you know, to keep the biscuits in the staff first-aid box. What if one of your staff needed a bandage, eh, Dr Matthews?'

'Then they'd look in the biscuit tin, of course, Dr Bickerbeak,' growled Dr Matthews.

Dr Bickerbeak eyed Dr Matthews angrily. He

noticed how noisily Dr Matthews sipped his tea and sat with his hind-paws up on the table. Dr Bickerbeak saw that a number of changes were necessary at Hilltop. He promised himself to have made those changes by Christmas.

Dr Matthews was a very good doctor and cared about his patients. It was true, though – there were certain parts of his job that he didn't pay careful attention to. These were exactly the things Dr Bickerbeak particularly noticed.

As he walked round the wards those first few days,

Dr Bickerbeak's sharp little eyes saw that windows weren't always sparkling, that the nurses weren't always keeping their medicine cupboards stocked up, and most of all, he noticed how much waste there was – of bandages, food, ointments. Even of electricity, he felt.

On the morning of Christmas Eve, Dr Matthews came on to the ward. Despite his fur, a shiver ran all the way down his body, right to the end of his tail.

'Anything the matter, Dr Matthews?' Dr Bickerbeak asked.

'I just think it's a bit chilly in the ward. We must make sure the patients don't get cold.'

'*I'm* not cold,' said Dr Bickerbeak, rustling his feathers. 'In fact, Matthews, as soon as I came in this morning I noticed how over-heated the ward was. Oh yes. *Far* too hot. No wonder the electricity bill's so high. So I turned the heating down.'

'But weren't you hot in the ward, Dr Bickerbeak,

because you'd just come in from outside where it's cold?'

'It's not cold outside! It's like summer,' insisted Dr Bickerbeak.

'I don't think it's *quite* like summer outside, Dr Bickerbeak,' answered Dr Matthews, looking out of the window. 'For instance, look at that snow storm. You don't get snow storms in the summer. You get them in mid-winter. Winter, Dr Bickerbeak. Traditionally the coldest time of year. When bears hibernate, and *birds* fly off to other countries because it's so cold.'

Dr Bickerbeak flapped his wings, turned up his beak and continued his ward round.

Dr Matthews soon noticed other changes. To begin with, no Christmas decorations had been put up in the wards this year, or even in the staff room. And then he opened the first-aid box and found it full of – *bandages*. Finally, when he did his ward round he heard the patients complaining about the hospital food.

'What's the matter with it?' he asked.

'It's cold, Dr Matthews. Cold breakfast, cold lunch, cold dinner.'

'Cold wards and cold food. At this rate,' Dr Matthews finished up, 'some patient is bound to catch a chill.'

And just at that moment, from the other end of the ward, he heard a cough.

Snow was caking the windowsills. Beyond the windows was more whiteness; no road, no trees, no valley – only fluffy snow. It looked very cold outside; it wasn't much warmer inside. The only ones who were warm were Dr Matthews and Dr Bickerbeak. They were in the medicine store-room and their blood was boiling.

'If it wasn't for you turning off the heating and insisting on cold meals, Geraldine wouldn't *have* a cough and a sore throat,' said Dr Matthews.

'And if you organised your medicine supply properly,' twittered Dr Bickerbeak, as he, Nurse Kitty and Dr Matthews searched shelf after shelf of medicine bottles, 'we would have some cough mixture to give to her. I mean, it's ridiculous not having a single bottle of cough mixture in a hospital.'

'Well,' confessed Dr Matthews, 'it didn't seem to be important. After all, you don't go to hospital because of a sore throat. It's not usually a big problem.'

'Not usually, no, Dr Matthews. Having a sore throat may be a small problem for some. But for others, like Geraldine, it's a big problem. A very big problem indeed.'

Puffing up his feathers, Dr Bickerbeak, hopped

back to the ward for a further inspection of Geraldine's throat. He climbed the step-ladder set up by her bed and shone his pen-torch into her open mouth.

When Dr Bickerbeak had gone Nurse Kitty looked sadly at Dr Matthews, who was gazing guiltily out of the window.

'If only the Teds could go and get some cough medicine from another hospital,' Kitty said.

'Not in this storm,' said Dr Matthews, shaking his head.

'But wait! I have an idea, Dr Matthews! Cough medicine is a mixture, isn't it?'

'Yes.'

'Well, maybe we can't get the medicine itself from another hospital, but we might have all the ingredients for the mixture here. Clare and

Arthur could
mix them up!'

Dr Matthews
thought for a
moment, then
suddenly wagged
his tail. 'Kitty,
you're an angel!'

Kitty purred and
felt warm inside,
despite the cold.

In the lab, Clare and
Arthur had all the Bunsen
burners flaring to keep themselves warm.
The effect was very Christmassy: bottles filled with
purple, gold and turquoise liquids twinkled in the
yellow light. Clare and Arthur were busy making the
very special Christmas cake which they made every
year to a secret formula. They were just about to beat
together the ingredients when Dr Matthews rushed
in.

'Stop!' he cried. 'We need your help right away.'

'But this is the most important moment in the
cake-making,' Arthur squeaked. 'We have to pay
close attention to the mixing. It's a very delicate
scientific process, Dr Matthews. And if we don't
make the cake now, it'll never be ready in time.'

'I'm sorry, Arthur. But we need you to make some
cough medicine for Geraldine. The patient must
always come first.'

'It's true, Arthur,' Clare agreed, her flour-covered whiskers drooping sadly.

'I suppose so,' admitted Arthur. His whiskers drooped too.

Dr Matthews left, feeling even more guilty.

'I only came in for an ingrowing hoof-nail,' coughed Geraldine. Every time she coughed, Dr Matthews and Dr Bickerbeak could see the pain, like a golf ball, running all the way down her neck. 'And now my throat's so sore I can't swallow anything.'

'Don't worry,' snorted Claude Curlytail, a little pig who was lying in the next bed. 'There's nothing worth swallowing here anyway. Just cold food. Still, I've heard they serve a delicious Christmas cake. At least that's *something* to look forward to tomorrow.'

Dr Matthews's tail fell when he heard this. It hardly rose when the lab mice appeared with a glass bottle of dark red syrup.

'There!' squeaked Arthur, as he triumphantly put the bottle down on the bedside table, adding, with surprising good humour, 'And a happy Christmas to you, Dr Matthews.'

Dr Matthews picked up the bottle with delight and gave it to Dr Bickerbeak, saying, 'And happy Christmas to *you*, Dr Bickerbeak.'

'Hmm. Better late than never, I suppose,' Dr Bickerbeak said.

'Well, if you hadn't turned off the heating – '

'And if you'd kept a check on – '

'Excuse me, doctors,' said a timid, throaty voice

above them. 'Sorry to interrupt but do you mind if I have a drop of that stuff? You never know, it might make my Christmas just a little happier . . .'

Dr Bickerbeak turned from Dr Matthews and hopped up the ladder.

It was Christmas morning.

Dr Matthews had spent the night at Hilltop because of the snow storm. As he woke up he thought he must be at home, because he was warm. Someone had turned the heating up. He dressed quickly, putting on his spare clean white coat, and hurried to the main ward.

The ward was warm too. It glittered with blue and yellow and crimson tinsel. At the far end a large Christmas tree sparkled with fairy lights.

'Who did all this?' Dr Matthews asked Claude Curlytail, who was finishing a delicious breakfast of hot porridge.

'Dr Bickerbeak. He was at it all night while we were asleep.'

Just at that moment, Dr Bickerbeak, who had slept at Hilltop too, wandered into the medicine store-room and found it perfectly tidy. All the bottles and packets were neatly arranged in the cupboards.

'Who did this?'

'Dr Matthews,' Nurse Kitty purred. 'He did it all night while we were asleep.'

It wasn't until lunch time that the two doctors met. And what a lunch it was: nut roast, potatoes, carrots, brussel sprouts, Christmas pudding, mince pies and custard – and all of it hot. There was one long table in the main ward for all the patients and staff. Dr Matthews and Dr Bickerbeak were seated next to each other.

'Well, I owe you an apology – ' began Dr Bickerbeak.

'No, no, no. *I* owe *you* one,' answered Dr Matthews.

'No, I insist – '

'Dr Bickerbeak . . . let's not argue about it,' Dr Matthews sighed.

'Pity about the cake though,' Dr Atticus remarked after the meal.

'Mmm. Pity about the cake,' agreed Surgeon Sally. 'Always looked forward to the cake.'

'What's that about the cake?' squealed Claude Curlytail.

Just then the ward doors burst open. Clare and Arthur entered, carrying a gigantic Christmas cake. Everyone cheered.

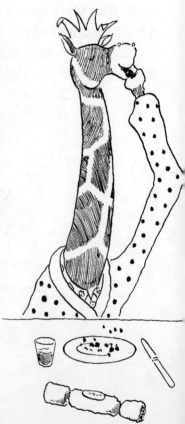

'But how did you make it in time?' Dr Matthews asked as they cut it into thick slices.

'Necessity is the mother of invention,' Arthur explained.

'Even in baking,' chipped in Clare.

'We discovered a new quick-acting formula,' continued Arthur. 'Now, who's going to try a piece first?'

'Me,' said a voice above them.

They all looked up at

Geraldine, whose throat, judging from the three-course lunch she'd just eaten, was cured.

'Delicious!' she said, after the first bite.

Slices were handed round until there was only one slice left for Dr Matthews and Dr Bickerbeak.

'Oh,' chirped Dr Bickerbeak.

'Oh,' sighed Dr Matthews. 'You have it, Dr Bickerbeak.'

'No, no. *You* have it, Dr Matthews.'

'No, no, no. I wouldn't like to – '

Just at that moment, Geraldine stepped forward, took the knife and cut the last piece of cake in half. Dr Matthews and Dr Bickerbeak both smiled, picked up a slice each and took a bite.

They both agreed with each other that it was the best Christmas cake either had ever tasted.

DR MATTHEWS AND NURSE KITTY GO ON HOLIDAY

Nurse Kitty thought a holiday would do Dr Matthews good. And she thought it would do even more good if she went with him.

'I still can't believe he agreed to go,' Kitty marvelled, as her flat-mate Tabitha helped her pack. 'And now we're on our way.'

'You're so lucky, Kitty. The Canary Isles too!'

'Oh, the taxi's here! Bye bye, Tabitha, I must hurry. Don't want to miss the flight.'

They hugged and entwined tails.

'You make sure that Dr Matthews relaxes. It sounds as if he never does,' urged Tabitha.

'Don't worry,' Kitty smiled. 'From now until we get back, we're both going to do *nothing* but relax.'

Dr Matthews had packed the previous evening. He got up early, had a shower, shook himself dry, and

ate a bowl of bone meal and
bran. Then he stood looking
out of the window, having
already checked and
double-checked that
the television, the
cooker and the lights
were switched off. He
thought of Hilltop
Hospital and how
Surgeon Sally
would cope
without him. It
was a pity she wasn't coming too. He imagined her
on the beach. Good strong swimmer, I bet, he
thought dreamily.

'Yoo-hoo!' Nurse Kitty was calling outside from
the window of the taxi.

They were on their way.

'And now, straight to the airport, please,' ordered
Kitty.

'Off on holiday, eh?' asked the driver, a fox, his red
brush quivering. 'Going anywhere nice?'

'The Canaries,' Kitty smiled.

'Canaries, eh? Luverly. Never been there meself. I
prefer the countryside,' he began. 'I – '

'And we don't want to miss the plane,' Kitty
interrupted.

'Don't worry! Won't take a minute. You see, this
early in the morning, all the roads are empty.'

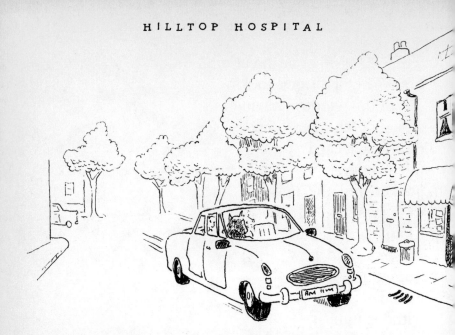

As they turned the corner a bright red sports car swerved quickly towards them, its horn blaring. It crashed straight into the taxi. For a moment there was an astonished silence.

'Kitty? Kitty? Are you all right?' Dr Matthews gently touched her shoulder.

'Oh yes, Dr Matthews. I'm fine.'

'What about you?' he asked the driver.

'*I'm* all right, but the driver of that sports car isn't – or he won't be in a minute. His mouth's about to get a pawful of fur.'

They all got out of the car. Dr Matthews hurried over to the sports car. Through the windscreen he saw the driver, a fat and warty toad, who looked a little green about the gills. He glared at Dr Matthews.

'Are you all right?' Dr Matthews called.

74

'Oh, I'm all right,' the toad croaked. 'My car isn't, though. And your driver won't be all right as soon as I get out. He's about to get a face full of flipper.'

The toad opened his door, then suddenly cried out.

'What's the matter?'

'My flipper!'

'What's the matter with it?'

'It's not working properly. And it's very painful!'

'Well, don't move it,' Dr Matthews insisted. 'Keep it perfectly still. It could be broken.'

'Who do you think you are, telling me what to do?' demanded the toad.

'I'm a doctor,' said Dr Matthews firmly.

75

'Oh.'

Dr Matthews turned to Nurse Kitty. 'We'll need an ambulance, Kitty.'

'Right, Dr Matthews.'

Nurse Kitty ran quickly to the phone box. She thought there was still time to get to the airport if the two Teds came immediately. Meanwhile, Dr Matthews tried to keep the two drivers from hitting each other.

'It's a good job you've got a broken flipper already,' said the cab-driver. 'Otherwise I would've had to have given you one.'

'It's a good job for you I've got a broken flipper. Otherwise I'd get out of this car and give *you* one. Fancy driving a car at that speed! Ooo, it makes me hopping mad.'

Soon they heard the siren of the ambulance as it wound its way through the empty streets. Suddenly it swerved round the corner, just missing the sports car, just missing the taxi, and stopping inches from a letter box.

'What time of the morning do you call this to 'ave an accident?' yawned Ted crossly as he got out of the ambulance.

'Yer, what time do you call this?' yawned the other Ted.

'I normally call it 6.30 am,' said the toad. 'What do you call it?'

'All right, all right,' barked Dr Matthews. The two Teds looked up in surprise.

'Dr Matthews! I thought you were on 'oliday,' said Ted.

'Yer, I thought you were supposed to be on 'oliday,' said the other Ted.

'We were on our way,' interrupted Nurse Kitty, adding anxiously, 'There's still time to get to the airport if we hurry.'

'Let's get the patient into the ambulance first,' Dr Matthews suggested. 'The stretchers, Teds.'

Dr Matthews, Nurse Kitty and the Teds lowered the toad down on to the stretcher. Although they did this with great care, it didn't stop the patient from croaking and whining, especially when Dr Matthews strapped the leg to the stretcher to keep it still.

'Well, you shouldn't drive so fast, should you?' said Ted.

'No concern for other road-users,' said the other Ted.

'There shouldn't've *been* any other road users at this time of the morning,' insisted the toad as they lifted him into the back of the ambulance. 'That's why I was trying out my new car. Then this idiot – '

The ambulance door slammed shut. For a moment the early morning street was peaceful once more.

Dr Matthews knew he had to make a decision then and there. He could leave the toad in the care of the Teds; then Kitty and he could continue their journey to the airport in another taxi. Or he could travel with the patient in the ambulance to make sure he arrived at the hospital safely. He didn't want to ruin their holiday, but then he thought how it would be ruined anyway if he spent the whole time worrying about his patient.

That was the sort of doctor Matthews was.

He told Nurse Kitty, 'I'm afraid, Kitty, you'll have to go on holiday by yourself. You'll still have time to get to the airport.'

A tear appeared in Kitty's eye as she heard this. She knew that if she went on holiday and didn't support Dr Matthews she would spend the whole week in the Canaries feeling guilty.

That was the sort of nurse Kitty was.

'I'm coming back to the hospital with you, Dr Matthews,' she said.

'You don't have to, Kitty.'

'Yes, Dr Matthews, I do.'

In silence, they put their cases in the ambulance, and then both stepped in themselves.

It was a bumpy ride to the hospital as the Teds drove at high speed, skidding around every corner. They almost ran over Dr Atticus, who'd just finished the night-shift and was very sleepy.

'Matthews? Kitty? I must be dreaming,' said Dr Atticus, raising his head from his shell. 'I thought you two were on holiday.'

'That's right. We were. And now we're not,' Dr Matthews declared.

'Yes, now we're not,' chimed Nurse Kitty sadly.

Dr Matthews and Nurse Kitty followed the Teds into the hospital foyer. Clare and Arthur, the lab mice, were checking their needles

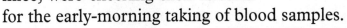

for the early-morning taking of blood samples.

'Dr Matthews! Kitty!' cried Clare. 'I thought you two were on holiday.'

'That's right. We were. And now we're not,' declared Dr Matthews.

'Yes, now we're not,' chimed Nurse Kitty, sniffing.

Dr Matthews and Nurse Kitty followed the two Teds and the stretcher into Casualty. There they found Surgeon Sally adjusting a drip.

'Matthews? Kitty? I thought you two were on holiday.'

'That's right, Sally. We were. And now we're not,' said Dr Matthews.

This time Nurse Kitty was too upset to say anything.

'We've got you another patient,' Dr Matthews stated in his most professional voice. 'Suspected broken flipper. Road accident.'

'Great,' said Surgeon Sally, rubbing her paws together. 'Let's have a look.'

While Dr Matthews and Nurse Kitty sat in the staff room drinking tea in silence, Surgeon Sally got to work on the patient's flipper. Having straightened it into the right position, Sally applied the bandages and plaster which when dry would form a cast around the flipper. This would keep the leg in position until it healed. Their patient was feeling much more comfortable in Sally's capable paws. He'd even stopped complaining.

'Now, what's this about that doctor and nurse not being on holiday when they're supposed to be?'

Sally told him.

'You mean it's all because of me? Little old me? Oh, this is terrible! Terrible! But why don't they just buy another ticket?'

'It's not as easy as that. Doctors and nurses don't earn as much as they should. They're not rich.'

'Aren't they? Well I am! Don't you know who I am? I'm Toad! Toad of Toad Hall! You must've heard of my great grandfather, surely? Someone wrote a book about him. Anyway, I have a private jet. I could get them to the Canaries just like that!' He snapped a flipper. 'No prob.'

'Are you serious?' Surgeon Sally asked. When she had seen how upset Dr Matthews was, even her surgeon's heart had softened. She realised she was really quite fond of Dr Matthews. In fact, she found she was fond enough to wonder if she *wanted* Dr Matthews to go on holiday at all, particularly with Nurse Kitty.

'Of course I'm serious. I'm Toad of Toad Hall, not some silly idiot! I mean what I say.'

Surgeon Sally paused for a moment. Then she picked up a wall-phone and made a call down to the staff room.

'Matthews? Sally here. Ring for a taxi. Your plane's waiting.'

In a large field behind Toad Hall, a small but sleek white jet glimmered in the August sunlight. Its engines were screaming. Nurse Kitty and Dr Matthews, the only passengers, were inside drinking champagne and eating exquisite Belgian biscuits; fish-flavoured for Kitty, bone-flavoured for Matthews. They felt the jet spring forward, speed up, and finally lift into the clear blue sky.

'Look, Dr Matthews!' said Kitty, pointing at the view beneath them. 'It's Hilltop Hospital. And there's Clare and Arthur and Dr Atticus waving at us. And . . . yes, Surgeon Sally's there too!'

Dr Matthews looked down and saw them all; he noticed Toad in a wheelchair. (Toad had wanted to fly the jet himself, but fortunately Surgeon Sally had insisted, 'Not with that flipper.') He relaxed back into his seat, but then suddenly thought of something. 'Did you see the two Teds, Kitty?'

'The Teds? No. But then *they* wouldn't bother making the effort to say goodbye. Or perhaps they were out on a call.'

'A *call!* A *call!* Then we'll have to turn back. We might be

needed. I'll tell the pilot at once!'

But before Dr Matthews could
release his safety-belt, Nurse Kitty
pointed a paw towards the hill ahead
of them. On the top of it they could
see a blue light flashing. As they
flew closer they could see the
light belonged to an
ambulance. Standing on
the roof of the
ambulance were the
two Teds. The
plane swooped
over them.

''Ave a good 'oliday!' the Teds roared and waved.
Then the jet, with Dr Matthews and Nurse Kitty
on board, was gone.

When Scottie first came to Hilltop Hospital he was afraid of injections. But he found they didn't hurt, and put up with them very bravely. Then he was worried he would hate the food, but discovered he quite liked it, especially the chocolate ice-cream. Then he was worried he would miss his mum and dad, but they visited every day and even brought him little presents; they made more of a fuss of him than when he was at home. So all that was left for him to miss was playing with his friends.

He sat there in bed with his ears drooped and his forelegs crossed.

'Cheer up, Scottie,' Nurse Kitty smiled, as she came to take his temperature. 'Only another week and you'll be going home.'

'But I want to go home *now*.'

'And what would you be doing at home?'

'I'd be out with my friends,' Scottie yapped

excitedly. 'We'd be off bone-hunting. Or racing and barking as loud as possible. We'd play the Sniffing Game. But it's boring here. There's no one to play with.'

It was true that the other patients didn't seem eager to get up and play. They lay or sat in bed, reading, sleeping, or listening to their radios with head-phones.

'Well, you'll have to amuse yourself then,' Nurse Kitty suggested.

But Scottie could only amuse himself by thinking about how miserable he was. In fact, he was so wrapped up in himself, he didn't notice the three things that happened next. Firstly, a bed, pushed by the two Teds, shot from one end of the ward to the other and out through the swing doors. Then, Scottie half-heard a familiar voice, but even so paid no attention to it. And lastly, a new patient arrived.

The two Teds wheeled the patient in on a trolley followed by Dr Matthews and Nurse Kitty. They

transferred the patient to the bed, pulled the curtain
round and left. The new arrival was sitting up in bed
just opposite Scottie. Everyone else stared curiously,
but there wasn't much to see as whatever it was had
its head completely wrapped in white bandages.

Just then Mrs Bifocal, a motherly earthworm,
entered the ward with her mobile library. In fact, she
almost collided with the bed, pushed by the two
Teds, which was whizzing back the way it had come.

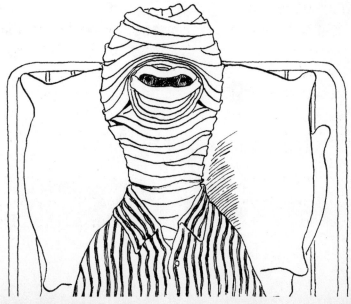

Mrs Bifocal was very proud of her library. It was just like an ordinary library, but all the books were stacked on a small cart, which could be pushed from bed to bed. So instead of the patient visiting the library, the library visited the patient.

Mrs Bifocal loved books. For her they were amazing things which, once opened, could whisk her away, like a magic carpet, to places she had never been. Behind her little round glasses was a powerful brain which remembered every book on her library shelves. As soon as she knew what kind of book a patient liked, she knew exactly where to look.

'And what kind of book do *you* like to read?' she asked, as she slid up to Scottie's bed.

'Books about bones,' Scottie said, thinking she wouldn't have any.

Instantly, Mrs Bifocal took out a book about

skeletons.

'Anything else?' she asked.

'What else is there?'

'Oh, there are space stories, pirate stories, ghost stories, cowboy stories – '

'Have you got any books on how to escape from hospital?'

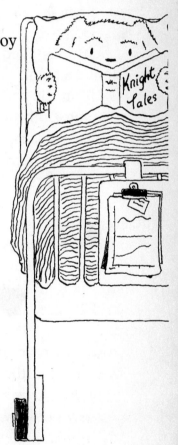

For once Mrs Bifocal was stumped. Then she remembered a book about knights in armour. 'I haven't got one about escaping from hospital, but I do have one about escaping from a castle dungeon.'

Scottie thought being in hospital was much like being locked in a dungeon, so when Mrs Bifocal slipped away, he picked up the second book she'd left, and began to read it. If he could escape from hospital, he thought, he could go out and play with his friends.

It wasn't long before he became fascinated with the story he was reading:

Every day and every evening, Sir Lionheart watched from the dungeon window all that went on in the castle courtyard. He noticed what times the guards changed, and which guards fell to sleep. He saw where the stables were and which horses were the strongest. After a week he knew more about castle life than the evil duke whose castle it was.

From this knowledge he planned his escape.

Scottie looked up. He imagined himself as Sir Lionheart and thought how, if he kept a careful watch on the ward, he too would work out a way of escaping from the hospital. Just then he heard that familiar voice again. He glanced down the ward, but saw no one he recognised. He knew he had to find out who it was.

All that day and evening, Scottie noticed everything that went on in the ward. He saw how, at 6 am the nurses on the night-shift changed with those on the day-shift. He noticed at what time the nurses took the patients' blood pressure and temperature, and at what time they made the beds. He learned to tell exactly when Mrs Fielding was about to enter the ward with her squeaky trolley, when Dr Matthews did his ward round, and when Clare and Arthur arrived to take blood for testing. He noticed too which patients were taken for X-rays and which patients had the most visitors in the

afternoon. The more he noticed the more interested
he became.

'Nurse Kitty,' he said one morning, as the bed,
which whizzed from one end of the ward to the
other, whizzed past once more. 'Why does that bed
keep whizzing up and down the ward?'

'That's Rachel Rabbit. She's expecting her babies.

All fifteen of them. Each
times she thinks she's ready,
the Teds rush her to the
theatre. But when she gets
there she finds she's not
ready after all.'

Once Scottie had started
asking questions he found he
couldn't stop. He asked why
Cathy Caterpillar in Bed
Four needed twenty meals a

day. Why Thomas Toad
had to have a bath every
half hour. Why Tony Ant
had to march up and
down the ward all the
time. And what *was* that
smell which came from
behind the curtain of
Bed Twenty-Seven?

'Perhaps,' suggested
Nurse Kitty, who had
enough to do without

answering countless questions, 'you should ask the patients themselves.'

And so Scottie began talking to the patients. He found out that Cathy needed so much food to give her the energy to turn into a butterfly. Thomas Toad

needed a bath every half hour to keep his skin damp, and Tony Ant marched up and down because that's what he always did at home. The more Scottie talked the more he wondered if he really wanted to escape after all. But, thinking of his friends outside, he decided to continue his plan.

There was one more thing he needed to know – could the patient in the bed opposite, wrapped in bandages, see or not? It was important to know as he or she might raise the alarm when Scottie escaped.

So Scottie went to find out. 'Hallo,' he said.

'Hallo.'

'Can you see me?'

'Course I can't. My eyes are covered in bandages. I can only hear. And I don't think I can even do that properly. I keep hearing this familiar voice and yet I don't know anyone here.'

'That's funny,' said Scottie, 'I keep hearing a familiar voice too.'

'In fact,' the patient said, cocking his head, 'I can

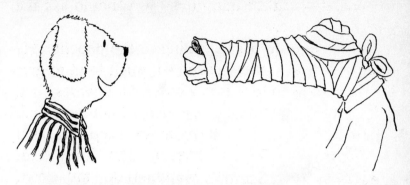

hear it now. It's *your* voice.'

'And I can hear it now too,' Scottie agreed. 'It's *your* voice.'

'Who are you?' asked the patient, turning his face towards Scottie, even though he couldn't see.

'My name's Scottie.'

'Scottie! It's me Allie! Allie Alligator.'

'Allie! What're you doing here?'

Allie was one of Scottie's school friends. He explained he was in hospital because he had a skin complaint. 'But it's so boring here,' Allie moaned. 'Especially if you can't see.'

'*Boring?*' Scottie said. 'It's not boring. It's really interesting in the ward, especially if you talk to the patients.'

So Scottie sat down and told Allie everything that was going on in the ward. He told him about the staff, Mrs Bifocal's mobile library, Mrs Fielding's squeaky tea-trolley, and why Cathy Caterpillar had to have twenty meals a day. Soon Allie was as interested in the ward as his friend. He even asked questions like, 'And what *is* that smell coming from the end of the ward?' and Scottie was able to tell him.

By the time he had finished describing all that went on in the ward, Scottie had completely forgotten about his plan to escape.

He soon found, in fact, that he had a new problem – he didn't ever want to leave.

A few days later, Scottie's mum and dad brought a small suitcase. Inside were some clean clothes to change into. Scottie filled the case with his toothbrush, his blue towel, face-flannel, soap-dish, pyjamas and slippers, his favourite bone and all his presents. It was time to go home.

When the moment came he grew quite sad. He knew all the patients and staff by now – and all their stories. When Surgeon Sally, Dr Matthews, Dr Atticus, Nurse Kitty, Clare and Arthur, and even Mrs Fielding, came to say goodbye, his nose grew wet and sniffy. Finally Mrs Bifocal arrived to collect her books.

'I expect you'll be glad to be home,' she smiled.

'Well, yes . . .' Scottie frowned. 'But I want to know what's going to happen next.'

'Next?'

'Yes! I want to know if Rachel has all fifteen of her babies. And who's going to be the new patient in my bed?' There were many other new mysteries too. Why was the curtain drawn round Bed Four at 6 am each evening? And why was Nurse Kitty always so happy when Dr Matthews was on the ward? 'There

are so many things that are going to happen at Hilltop, and I won't know any of them.' Scottie looked sad. 'Allie's leaving tomorrow and he wants to know what's going to happen in Hilltop too.'

Mrs Bifocal was thoughtful for a moment. 'I know. I'll write down what happens. I'll make it into a little book, and when I've finished it, I'll send it to you.'

'Will you, Mrs Bifocal? Oh, thank you!'

So that's what Mrs Bifocal did. She called the book: